THE
BEATRIX POTTER
TREASURY

THE
BEATRIX POTTER

TREASURY

TM

F. WARNE & Cº

FREDERICK WARNE

Published by the Penguin Group
27 Wrights Lane, London W8 5TZ, England
Viking Penguin Inc., 40 West 23rd Street, New York, New York 10010, USA
Penguin Books Australia Ltd, Ringwood, Victoria, Australia
Penguin Books Canada Ltd, 2801 John Street, Markham, Ontario, Canada L3R 1B4
Penguin Books (NZ) Ltd, 182–190 Wairau Road, Auckland 10, New Zealand

Penguin Books Ltd, Registered Offices: Harmondsworth, Middlesex, England

First published 1988
This revised edition published 1990

Universal Copyright Notice:
Beatrix Potter's works included in this volume copyright ©
Frederick Warne & Co., 1902, 1903, 1907, 1913
Copyright in all countries signatory to the Berne Convention
New reproduction copyright 1987
Copyright in all countries signatory to the Berne and
Universal Conventions

All rights reserved. Without limiting the rights under copyright reserved
above, no part of this publication may be reproduced, stored in or
introduced into a retrieval system, or transmitted, in any form or by any means
(electronic, mechanical, photocopying, recording or otherwise), without the
prior written permission of both the copyright owner and the above publisher
of this book

ISBN 0 7232 3715 8

Printed and bound in Great Britain by
William Clowes Limited, Beccles and London

CONTENTS

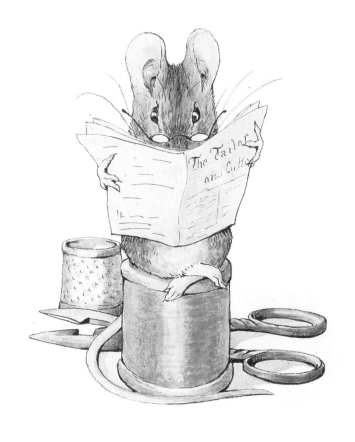

INTRODUCTION

These four delightful stories by Beatrix Potter have been enjoyed by children (and adults!) for generations. *The Tale of Peter Rabbit* is the first and best loved of Beatrix Potter's tales. Peter is a naughty rabbit and when he strays into Mr. McGregor's garden in search of lettuces he finds himself in all kinds of trouble, much to the dismay of Old Mrs. Rabbit, for Peter's father was put in a pie by Mrs. McGregor. Beatrix herself preferred *The Tailor of Gloucester* amongst all her stories. She heard the tale on a visit to her cousin, who lived near Gloucester: a tailor in the town left an unfinished waistcoat in his workshop on a Saturday, only to find it all ready, except for one button-hole, on the Monday. In reality, his assistants had finished the job, but how much jollier to imagine the work done by mice, sewing and singing on Christmas Eve. *The Tale of Tom Kitten* was published a few years later and by this time, Beatrix had bought Hill Top farm, in the Lake District. The house and its surroundings can be clearly recognized in several illustrations: Tom and his sisters lose their clothes in the garden at Hill Top, and their mother takes them off to the farmhouse to be washed and brushed. Finally, *The Tale of Pigling Bland* completes this enchanting collection. Pigling Bland and Alexander were two of Beatrix Potter's own pigs at Hill Top, and again, the farmyard appears in many of the illustrations. Pigling Bland and the little girl pig, Pigwig, manage to escape being made into bacon and hams, and together they dance 'over the hills and far away'.

THE TALE OF
PETER RABBIT

ONCE upon a time there were four little Rabbits, and their names were—

Flopsy,

Mopsy,

Cotton-tail,

and Peter.

They lived with their Mother in a sand-bank, underneath the root of a very big fir-tree.

'Now, my dears,' said old Mrs. Rabbit one morning, 'you may go into the fields or down the lane, but don't go into Mr. Mc-Gregor's garden: your Father had an accident there; he was put in a pie by Mrs. McGregor.'

'Now run along, and don't get into mischief. I am going out.'

Then old Mrs. Rabbit took a basket and her umbrella, and went through the wood to the baker's. She bought a loaf of brown bread and five currant buns.

Flopsy, Mopsy, and Cotton-tail, who were good little bunnies, went down the lane to gather blackberries:

But Peter, who was very naughty, ran straight away to Mr. McGregor's garden, and squeezed under the gate!

First he ate some lettuces and some French beans; and then he ate some radishes;

And then, feeling rather sick, he went to look for some parsley.

But round the end of a cucumber frame, whom should he meet but Mr. McGregor!

Mr. McGregor was on his hands and knees planting out young cabbages, but he jumped up and ran after Peter, waving a rake and calling out, 'Stop thief!'

Peter was most dreadfully frightened; he rushed all over the garden, for he had forgotten the way back to the gate.

He lost one of his shoes among the cabbages, and the other shoe amongst the potatoes.

After losing them, he ran on four legs and went faster, so that I think he might have got away altogether if he had not unfortunately run into a gooseberry net, and got caught by the large buttons on his jacket. It was a blue jacket with brass buttons, quite new.

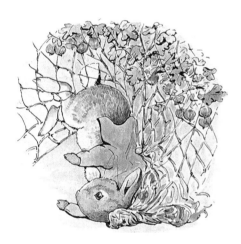

Peter gave himself up for lost, and shed big tears; but his sobs were overheard by some friendly sparrows, who flew to him in great excitement, and implored him to exert himself.

Mr. McGregor came up with a sieve, which he intended to pop upon the top of Peter; but Peter wriggled out just in time, leaving his jacket behind him.

And rushed into the tool-shed, and jumped into a can. It would have been a beautiful thing to hide in, if it had not had so much water in it.

Mr. McGregor was quite sure that Peter was somewhere in the tool-shed, perhaps hidden underneath a flower-pot. He began to turn them over carefully, looking under each.

Presently Peter sneezed—'Kertyschoo!' Mr. McGregor was after him in no time.

And tried to put his foot upon Peter, who jumped out of a window, upsetting three plants. The window was too small for Mr. McGregor, and he was tired of running after Peter. He went back to his work.

He found a door in a wall; but it was locked, and there was no room for a fat little rabbit to squeeze underneath.

An old mouse was running in and out over the stone doorstep, carrying peas and beans to her family in the wood. Peter asked her the way to the gate, but she had such a large pea in her mouth that she could not answer. She only shook her head at him. Peter began to cry.

Peter sat down to rest; he was out of breath and trembling with fright, and he had not the least idea which way to go. Also he was very damp with sitting in that can.

After a time he began to wander about, going lippity—lippity—not very fast, and looking all around.

Then he tried to find his way straight across the garden, but he became more and more puzzled. Presently, he came to a pond where Mr. McGregor filled his water-cans. A white cat was staring at some gold-fish, she sat very, very still, but now and then the tip of her tail twitched as if it were alive. Peter thought it best to go away without speaking to her; he had heard about cats from his cousin, little Benjamin Bunny.

He went back towards the tool-shed, but suddenly, quite close to him, he heard the noise of a hoe—scr-r-ritch, scratch, scratch, scritch. Peter scuttered underneath the bushes. But presently, as nothing happened, he came out, and climbed upon a wheelbarrow and peeped over. The first thing he saw was Mr. McGregor hoeing onions. His back was turned towards Peter, and beyond him was the gate!

Peter got down very quietly off the wheelbarrow, and started running as fast as he could go, along a straight walk behind some black-currant bushes.

Mr. McGregor caught sight of him at the corner, but Peter did not care. He slipped underneath the gate, and was safe at last in the wood outside the garden.

Mr. McGregor hung up the little jacket and the shoes for a scare-crow to frighten the blackbirds.

Peter never stopped running or looked behind him till he got home to the big fir-tree.

He was so tired that he flopped down upon the nice soft sand on the floor of the rabbit-hole and shut his eyes. His mother was busy cooking; she wondered what he had done with his clothes. It was the second little jacket and pair of shoes that Peter had lost in a fortnight!

I am sorry to say that Peter was not very well during the evening.

His mother put him to bed, and made some camomile tea; and she gave a dose of it to Peter!

'One table-spoonful to be taken at bed-time.'

But Flopsy, Mopsy, and Cotton-tail had bread and milk and blackberries for supper.

THE
TAILOR OF
GLOUCESTER

MY DEAR FREDA,

Because you are fond of fairy-tales, and have been ill, I have made you a story all for yourself—a new one that nobody has read before.

And the queerest thing about it is—that I heard it in Gloucestershire, and that it is true— at least about the tailor, the waistcoat, and the
'No more twist!'

Christmas, 1901

IN the time of swords and periwigs and full-skirted coats with flowered lappets—when gentlemen wore ruffles, and gold-laced waistcoats of paduasoy and taffeta—there lived a tailor in Gloucester.

He sat in the window of a little shop in Westgate Street, cross-legged on a table, from morning till dark.

All day long while the light lasted he sewed and snippeted, piecing out his satin and pompadour, and lutestring; stuffs had strange names, and were very expensive in the days of the Tailor of Gloucester.

But although he sewed fine silk for his neighbours, he himself was very, very poor—a little old man in spectacles, with a pinched face, old crooked fingers, and a suit of thread-bare clothes.

He cut his coats without waste, according to his embroidered cloth; they were very small ends and snippets that lay about upon the table—'Too narrow breadths for nought—except waistcoats for mice,' said the tailor.

One bitter cold day near Christmas-time the tailor began to make a coat—a coat of cherry-coloured corded silk embroidered with pansies and roses, and a cream coloured satin waistcoat—trimmed with gauze and green worsted chenille—for the Mayor of Gloucester.

The tailor worked and worked, and he talked to himself. He measured the silk, and turned it round and round, and trimmed it into shape with his shears; the table was all littered with cherry-coloured snippets.

'No breadth at all, and cut on the cross; it is no breadth at all; tippets for mice and ribbons for mobs! for mice!' said the Tailor of Gloucester.

When the snow-flakes came down against the small leaded window-panes and shut out the light, the tailor had done his day's work; all the silk and satin lay cut out upon the table.

There were twelve pieces for the coat and four pieces for the waistcoat; and there were pocket flaps and cuffs, and buttons all in order. For the lining of the coat there was fine yellow taffeta; and for the button-holes of the waistcoat, there was cherry-coloured twist. And everything was ready to sew together in the morning, all measured and sufficient—except that there was wanting just one single skein of cherry-coloured twisted silk.

The tailor came out of his shop at dark, for he did not sleep there at nights; he fastened the window and locked the door, and took away the key. No one lived there at night but little brown mice, and they run in and out without any keys!

For behind the wooden wainscots of all the old houses in Gloucester, there are little mouse staircases and secret trap-doors; and the mice run from house to house through those long

narrow passages; they can run all over the town without going into the streets.

But the tailor came out of his shop, and shuffled home through the snow. He lived quite near by in College Court, next the doorway to College Green; and although it was not a big house, the tailor was so poor he only rented the kitchen.

He lived alone with his cat; it was called Simpkin.

Now all day long while the tailor was out at work, Simpkin kept house by himself; and he also was fond of the mice, though he gave them no satin for coats!

'Miaw?' said the cat when the tailor opened the door. 'Miaw?'

The tailor replied—'Simpkin, we shall make our fortune, but I am worn to a ravelling. Take this groat (which is our last fourpence) and Simpkin, take a china pipkin; buy a penn'orth of bread, a penn'orth of milk and a penn'orth of sausages. And oh, Simpkin, with the last penny of our fourpence buy me one penn'orth of cherry-coloured silk. But do not lose the last penny of the fourpence, Simpkin, or I am undone and worn to a thread-paper, for I have NO MORE TWIST.'

Then Simpkin again

said, 'Miaw?' and took the groat and the pipkin, and went out into the dark.

The tailor was very tired and beginning to be ill. He sat down by the hearth and talked to himself about that wonderful coat.

'I shall make my fortune—to be cut bias—the Mayor of Gloucester is to be married on Christmas Day in the morning, and he hath ordered a coat and an embroidered waistcoat— to be lined with yellow taffeta—and the taffeta sufficeth; there is no more left over in snippets than will serve to make tippets for mice—'

Then the tailor started; for suddenly, interrupting him, from the dresser at the other side of the kitchen came a number of little noises—

Tip tap, tip tap, tip tap tip!

'Now what can that be?' said the Tailor of Gloucester, jumping up from his chair. The dresser was covered with crockery and pipkins, willow pattern plates, and tea-cups and mugs.

The tailor crossed the kitchen, and stood quite still beside the dresser, listening, and peering through his spectacles. Again from under a tea-cup, came those funny little noises—

Tip tap, tip tap, tip tap tip!

'This is very peculiar,' said the Tailor of Gloucester; and he lifted up the tea-cup which was upside down.

Out stepped a little live lady mouse, and made a curtsey to the tailor! Then she hopped away down off the dresser, and under the wainscot.

The tailor sat down again by the fire, warming his poor cold hands, and mumbling to himself—

'The waistcoat is cut out from peach-coloured satin—tambour stitch and rose-buds in beautiful floss silk. Was I wise to entrust my last fourpence to Simpkin? One-and-twenty button-holes of cherry-coloured twist!'

But all at once, from the dresser, there came other little noises:
Tip tap, tip tap, tip tap tip!

'This is passing extraordinary!' said the Tailor of Gloucester, and turned over another tea-cup, which was upside down.

Out stepped a little gentleman mouse, and made a bow to the tailor!

And then from all over the dresser came a chorus of little tappings, all sounding together, and answering one another, like watch-beetles in an old worm-eaten window-shutter—

Tip tap, tip tap, tip tap tip!

28

And out from under tea-cups and from under bowls and basins, stepped other and more little mice who hopped away down off the dresser and under the wainscot.

The tailor sat down, close over the fire, lamenting—'One-and-twenty button-holes of cherry-coloured silk! To be finished by noon of Saturday: and this is Tuesday evening. Was it right to let loose those mice, undoubtedly the property of Simpkin? Alack, I am undone, for I have no more twist!'

The little mice came out again, and listened to the tailor; they took notice of the pattern of that wonderful coat. They whispered to one another about the taffeta lining, and about little mouse tippets.

And then all at once they all ran away together down the passage behind the wainscot, squeaking and calling to one another, as they ran from house to house; and not one mouse was left in the tailor's kitchen when Simpkin came back with the pipkin of milk!

Simpkin opened the door and bounced in, with an angry 'G-r-r-miaw!' like a cat that is vexed: for he hated the snow, and there was snow in his ears, and snow in his collar at the back of his neck. He put down the loaf and the sausages upon the dresser, and sniffed.

'Simpkin,' said the tailor, 'where is my twist?'

But Simpkin set down the pipkin of milk upon the dresser, and looked suspiciously at the tea-cups. He wanted his supper of little fat mouse!

'Simpkin,' said the tailor, 'where is my TWIST?'

But Simpkin hid a little parcel privately in the tea-pot, and spit and growled at the tailor; and if Simpkin had been able to talk, he would have asked: 'Where is my MOUSE?'

'Alack, I am undone!' said the Tailor of Gloucester, and went sadly to bed.

All that night long Simpkin hunted and searched through the kitchen, peeping into cupboards and under the wainscot, and into the tea-pot where he had hidden that twist; but still he found never a mouse!

Whenever the tailor muttered and talked in his sleep, Simpkin said 'Miaw-ger-r-w-s-s-ch!' and made strange horrid noises, as cats do at night.

For the poor old tailor was very ill with a fever, tossing and turning in his four-post bed; and still in his dreams he mumbled—

'No more twist! no more twist!'

All that day he was ill, and the next day, and the next; and what should become of the cherry-coloured coat? In the tailor's shop in Westgate Street the embroidered silk and satin lay cut out upon the table—one-and-twenty button-holes—and who should come to sew them, when the window was barred, and the door was fast locked?

But that does not hinder the little brown mice; they run in and out without any keys through all the old houses in Gloucester!

Out of doors the market folks went trudging through the snow to buy their geese and turkeys, and to bake their Christmas pies; but there would be no Christmas dinner for Simpkin and the poor old Tailor of Gloucester.

The tailor lay ill for three days and nights; and then it was Christmas Eve, and very late at night. The moon climbed up over the roofs and chimneys, and looked down over the gateway into College Court. There were no lights in the windows, nor any sound in the houses; all the city of Gloucester was fast asleep under the snow.

And still Simpkin wanted his mice, and he mewed as he stood beside the four-post bed.

But it is in the old story that all the beasts can talk, in the night between Christmas Eve and Christmas Day in the morning (though there are very few folk that can hear them, or know what it is that they say).

When the Cathedral clock struck twelve there was an answer—like an echo of the chimes—and Simpkin heard it, and came out of the tailor's door, and wandered about in the snow.

From all the roofs and gables and old wooden houses in Gloucester came a thousand merry voices singing the old Christmas rhymes—all the old songs that ever I heard of, and some that I don't know, like Whittington's bells.

First and loudest the cocks cried out: 'Dame, get up, and bake your pies!'

'Oh, dilly, dilly, dilly!' sighed Simpkin.

And now in a garret there were lights and sounds of dancing, and cats came from over the way.

'Hey, diddle, diddle, the cat and the fiddle! All the cats in Gloucester—except me,' said Simpkin.

Under the wooden eaves the starlings and sparrows sang of Christmas pies; the jack-daws woke up in the Cathedral tower; and although it was the middle of the night the throstles and robins sang; the air was quite full of little twittering tunes.

But it was all rather provoking to poor hungry Simpkin!

Particularly he was vexed with some little shrill voices from behind a wooden lattice. I think that they were bats, because they always have very small voices—especially in a black frost, when they talk in their sleep, like the Tailor of Gloucester.

They said something mysterious that sounded like—

'Buz, quoth the blue fly; hum, quoth the bee;
Buz and hum they cry, and so do we!'

and Simpkin went away shaking his ears as if he had a bee in his bonnet.

From the tailor's shop in Westgate came a glow of light; and when Simpkin crept up to peep in at the window it was full of candles. There was a snippeting of scissors, and snappeting of thread; and little mouse voices sang loudly and gaily—

'Four-and-twenty tailors
Went to catch a snail,
The best man amongst them
Durst not touch her tail;
She put out her horns
Like a little kyloe cow,
Run, tailors, run! or she'll have you all e'en now!'

Then without a pause the little mouse voices went on again—

'Sieve my lady's oatmeal,
Grind my lady's flour,
Put it in a chestnut,
Let it stand an hour—'

'Mew! Mew!' interrupted Simpkin, and he scratched at the door. But the key was under the tailor's pillow, he could not get in.

The little mice only laughed, and tried another tune—

'Three little mice sat down to spin,
Pussy passed by and she peeped in.
What are you at, my fine little men?
Making coats for gentlemen.
Shall I come in and cut off your threads?
Oh, no, Miss Pussy, you'd bite off our heads!'

'Mew! Mew!' cried Simpkin. 'Hey diddle dinketty?' answered the little mice—

'Hey diddle dinketty, poppetty pet!
The merchants of London they wear scarlet;
Silk in the collar, and gold in the hem,
So merrily march the merchantmen!'

They clicked their thimbles to mark the time, but none of the songs pleased Simpkin; he sniffed and mewed at the door of the shop.

'And then I bought
A pipkin and a popkin,
A slipkin and a slopkin,
All for one farthing—

and upon the kitchen dresser!' added the rude little mice.

'Mew! scratch! scratch!' scuffled Simpkin on the window-sill; while the little mice inside sprang to their feet, and all began to shout at once in little twittering voices: 'No more twist! No more twist!' And they barred up the window shutters and shut out Simpkin.

But still through the nicks in the shutters he could hear the click of thimbles, and little mouse voices singing—

'No more twist! No more twist!'

Simpkin came away from the shop and went home, considering in his mind. He found the poor old tailor without fever, sleeping peacefully.

Then Simpkin went on tip-toe and took a little parcel of silk out of the tea-pot, and looked at it in the moonlight; and he felt quite ashamed of his badness compared with those good little mice!

When the tailor awoke in the morning, the first thing which he saw upon the patchwork quilt, was a skein of cherry-coloured twisted silk, and beside his bed stood the repentant Simpkin!

'Alack, I am worn to a ravelling,' said the Tailor of Gloucester, 'but I have my twist!'

The sun was shining on the snow when the tailor got up and dressed, and came out into the street with Simpkin running before him.

The starlings whistled on the chimney stacks, and the throstles and robins sang—but they sang their own little noises, not the words they had sung in the night.

'Alack,' said the tailor, 'I have my twist; but no more strength—nor time—than will serve to make me one single button-hole; for this is Christmas Day in the Morning! The Mayor of Gloucester shall be married by noon—and where is his cherry-coloured coat?'

He unlocked the door of the little shop in Westgate Street, and Simpkin ran in, like a cat that expects something.

But there was no one there! Not even one little brown mouse!

The boards were swept clean; the little ends of thread and the little silk snippets were all tidied away, and gone from off the floor.

But upon the table—oh joy! the tailor gave a shout—there, where he had left plain cuttings of silk—there lay the most beautifullest coat and embroidered satin waistcoat that ever were worn by a Mayor of Gloucester.

There were roses and pansies upon the facings of the coat; and the waistcoat was worked with poppies and corn-flowers.

Everything was finished except just one single cherry-coloured button-hole, and where that button-hole was wanting there was pinned a scrap of paper with these words—in little teeny weeny writing—

NO MORE TWIST

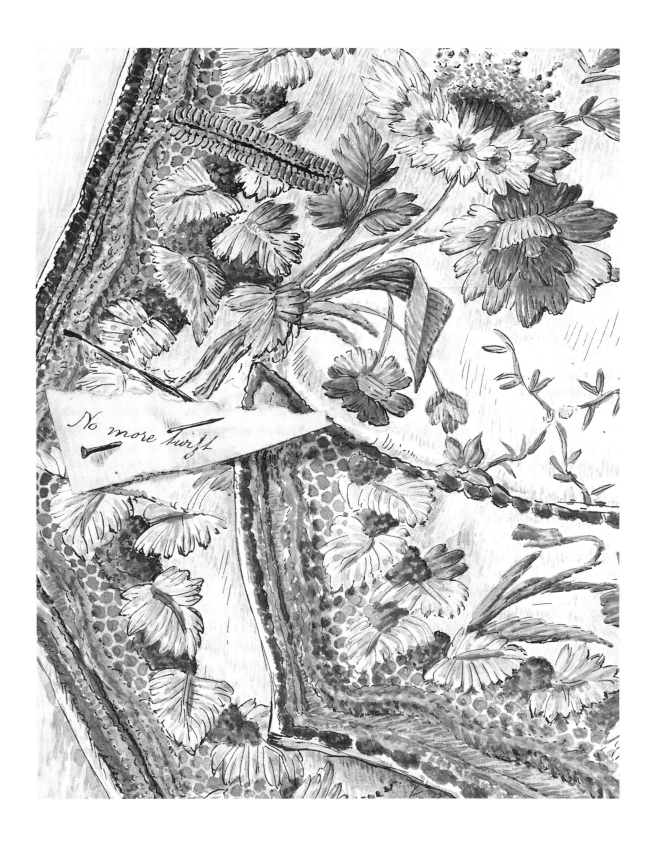

And from then began the luck of the Tailor of Gloucester; he grew quite stout, and he grew quite rich.

He made the most wonderful waistcoats for all the rich merchants of Gloucester, and for all the fine gentlemen of the country round.

Never were seen such ruffles, or such embroidered cuffs and lappets! But his button-holes were the greatest triumph of it all.

The stitches of those button-holes were so neat—*so* neat—I wonder how they could be stitched by an old man in spectacles, with crooked old fingers, and a tailor's thimble.

The stitches of those button-holes were so small—*so* small— they looked as if they had been made by little mice!

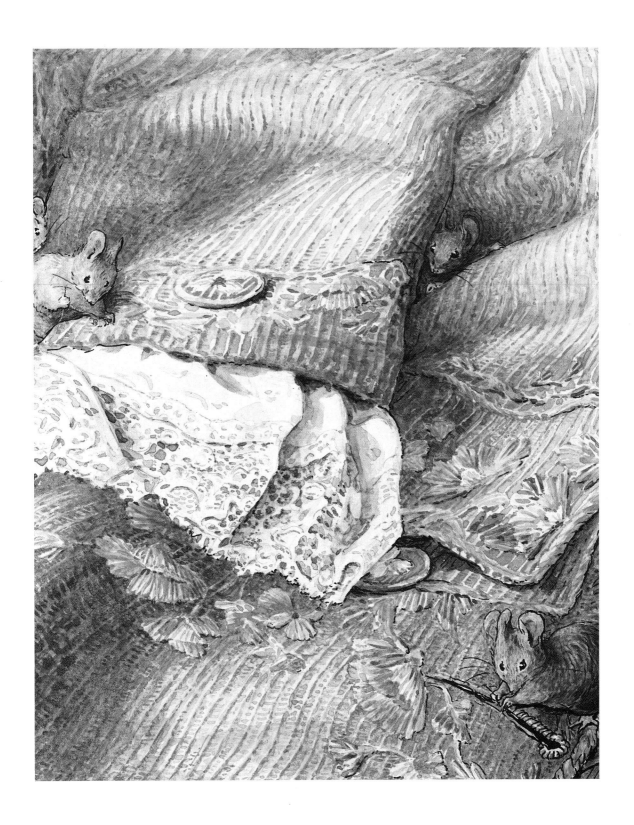

THE TALE OF
TOM KITTEN

Dedicated
to all
PICKLES,
—especially to those that
get upon my garden wall

ONCE upon a time there were three little kittens, and their names were Mittens, Tom Kitten, and Moppet.

They had dear little fur coats of their own; and they tumbled about the doorstep and played in the dust.

But one day their mother —Mrs. Tabitha Twitchit—expected friends to tea ; so she fetched the kittens indoors, to wash and dress them, before the fine company arrived.

First she scrubbed their faces (this one is Moppet).

Then she brushed their fur, (this one is Mittens).

Then she combed their tails and whiskers (this is Tom Kitten).

Tom was very naughty, and he scratched.

Mrs. Tabitha dressed Moppet and Mittens in clean pinafores and tuckers; and then she took all sorts of elegant uncomfortable clothes out of a chest of drawers, in order to dress up her son Thomas.

Tom Kitten was very fat, and he had grown; several buttons burst off. His mother sewed them on again.

When the three kittens were ready, Mrs. Tabitha unwisely turned them out into the garden, to be out of the way while she made hot buttered toast.

'Now keep your frocks clean, children! You must walk on your hind legs. Keep away from the dirty ash-pit, and from Sally Henny Penny, and from the pig-stye and the Puddle-Ducks.'

Moppet and Mittens walked down the garden path unsteadily. Presently they trod upon their pinafores and fell on their noses.

When they stood up there were several green smears!

'Let us climb up the rockery, and sit on the garden wall,' said Moppet.

They turned their pinafores back to front, and went up with a skip and a jump; Moppet's white tucker fell down into the road.

Tom Kitten was quite unable to jump when walking upon his hind legs in trousers. He came up the rockery by degrees, breaking the ferns, and shedding buttons right and left.

He was all in pieces when he reached the top of the wall.

Moppet and Mittens tried to pull him together; his hat fell off, and the rest of his buttons burst.

While they were in difficulties, there was a pit pat paddle pat! and the three Puddle-Ducks came along the hard high road, marching one behind the other and doing the goose-step— pit pat paddle pat! pit pat waddle pat!

They stopped and stood in a row, and stared up at the kittens. They had very small eyes and looked surprised.

Then the two duck-birds, Rebeccah and Jemima Puddle-Duck, picked up the hat and tucker and put them on.

Mittens laughed so that she fell off the wall. Moppet and Tom descended after her; the pinafores and all the rest of Tom's clothes came off on the way down.

'Come! Mr. Drake Puddle-Duck,' said Moppet—'Come and help us to dress him! Come and button up Tom!'

Mr. Drake Puddle-Duck advanced in a slow sideways manner, and picked up the various articles.

But he put them on *himself!* They fitted him even worse than Tom Kitten.

'It's a very fine morning!' said Mr. Drake Puddle-Duck.

And he and Jemima and Rebeccah Puddle-Duck set off up the road, keeping step—pit pat, paddle pat! pit pat, waddle pat!

Then Tabitha Twitchit came down the garden and found her kittens on the wall with no clothes on.

She pulled them off the wall, smacked them, and took them back to the house.

'My friends will arrive in a minute, and you are not fit to be seen; I am affronted,' said Mrs. Tabitha Twitchit.

She sent them upstairs; and I am sorry to say she told her friends that they were in bed with the measles; which was not true.

Quite the contrary; they were not in bed: *not* in the least.

Somehow there were very extraordinary noises over-head, which disturbed the dignity and repose of the tea party.

And I think that some day I shall have to make another, larger, book, to tell you more about Tom Kitten!

As for the Puddle-Ducks—they went into a pond.

The clothes all came off directly, because there were no buttons.

And Mr. Drake Puddle-Duck, and Jemima and Rebeccah, have been looking for them ever since.

THE TALE OF
PIGLING BLAND

For
Cecily and Charlie

A Tale of
The Christmas Pig

ONCE upon a time there was an old pig called Aunt Pettitoes. She had eight of a family: four little girl pigs, called Crosspatch, Suck-suck, Yock-yock and Spot; and four little boy pigs, called Alexander, Pigling Bland, Chin-chin and Stumpy. Stumpy had had an accident to his tail.

The eight little pigs had very fine appetites. 'Yus, yus, yus! they eat and indeed they *do* eat!' said Aunt Pettitoes, looking at her family with pride. Suddenly there were fearful squeals; Alexander had squeezed inside the hoops of the pig trough and stuck.

Aunt Pettitoes and I dragged him out by the hind legs.

Chin-chin was already in disgrace; it was washing day, and he had eaten a piece of soap. And presently in a basket of clean clothes, we found another dirty little pig.

'Tchut, tut, tut! whichever is this?' grunted Aunt Pettitoes. Now all the pig family are pink, or pink with black spots, but this pig child was smutty black all over; when it had been popped into a tub, it proved to be Yock-yock.

I went into the garden; there I found Cross-patch and Suck-suck rooting up carrots. I whipped them myself and led them out by the ears. Cross-patch tried to bite me.

'Aunt Pettitoes, Aunt Pettitoes! you are a worthy person, but your family is not well brought up. Every one of them has been in mischief except Spot and Pigling Bland.'

'Yus, yus!' sighed Aunt Pettitoes. 'And they drink bucketfuls of milk; I shall have to get another cow! Good little Spot shall stay at home to do the housework; but the others must go. Four little boy pigs and four little girl pigs are too many altogether.' 'Yus, yus, yus,' said Aunt Pettitoes, 'there will be more to eat without them.'

So Chin-chin and Suck-suck went away in a wheelbarrow, and Stumpy, Yock-yock and Cross-patch rode away in a cart.

And the other two little boy pigs, Pigling Bland and Alexander, went to market. We brushed their coats, we curled their tails and washed their little faces, and wished them good-bye in the yard.

Aunt Pettitoes wiped her eyes with a large pocket handkerchief, then she wiped Pigling Bland's nose and shed tears; then she wiped Alexander's nose and shed tears; then she passed the handkerchief to Spot. Aunt Pettitoes sighed and grunted, and addressed those little pigs as follows:

'Now Pigling Bland, son Pigling bland, you must go to market. Take your brother Alexander by the hand. Mind your Sunday clothes, and remember to blow your nose '—(Aunt Pettitoes passed

round the handkerchief again)—'beware of traps, hen roosts, bacon and eggs; always walk upon your hind legs.' Pigling Bland, who was a sedate little pig, looked solemnly at his mother, a tear trickled down his cheek.

Aunt Pettitoes turned to

the other—'Now son Alexander take the hand'—'Wee, wee, wee!' giggled Alexander—'take the hand of your brother Pigling Bland, you must go to market. Mind—' 'Wee, wee, wee!' interrupted Alexander again. 'You put me out,' said Aunt Pettitoes—'Observe sign-posts and milestones; do not gobble herring bones—' 'And remember,' said I impressively, 'if you once cross the county boundary you cannot come back. Alexander, you are not attending. Here are two licences permitting two pigs to go to market in Lancashire. Attend, Alexander. I have had no end of trouble in getting these papers from the policeman.' Pigling Bland listened

gravely; Alexander was hopelessly volatile.

I pinned the papers, for safety, inside their waistcoat pockets; Aunt Pettitoes gave to each a little bundle, and eight conversation peppermints with appropriate

moral sentiments in screws of paper. Then they started.

Pigling Bland and Alexander trotted along steadily for a mile; at least Pigling Bland did. Alexander made the road half as long again by skipping from side to side. He danced about and pinched his brother, singing—

'This pig went to market,
    this pig stayed at home,
This pig had a bit of meat—

let's see what they have given *us* for dinner, Pigling?'

Pigling Bland and Alexander sat down and untied their bundles. Alexander gobbled up his dinner in no time; he had already eaten all his own peppermints. 'Give me one of yours, please, Pigling.' 'But I wish to preserve them for emergencies,' said Pigling Bland doubtfully. Alexander went into squeals of laughter. Then he pricked Pigling with the pin that had fastened his pig paper; and when Pigling slapped him he dropped the pin, and tried to take Pigling's pin, and the papers got mixed up. Pigling Bland reproved Alexander.

But presently they made it up again, and trotted away together, singing—

> 'Tom, Tom, the piper's son, stole a pig and away he ran!
> But all the tune that he could play, was "Over the hills and far away!"'

'What's that, young sirs? Stole a pig? Where are your licences?' said the policeman. They had nearly run against him round a corner. Pigling Bland pulled out his paper; Alexander, after fumbling, handed over something scrumply—

'To $2\frac{1}{2}$ oz. conversation sweeties at three far-things'—'What's this? This ain't a licence.' Alexander's nose lengthened visibly, he had lost it. 'I had one, indeed I had, Mr. Police-man!'

'It's not likely they let you start without. I am passing the farm. You may walk with me.' 'Can I come back too?' inquired

Pigling Bland. 'I see no reason, young sir; your paper is all right.'
Pigling Bland did not like going on alone, and it was beginning
to rain. But it is unwise to argue with the police; he gave his
brother a peppermint, and watched him out of sight.

To conclude the adventures of Alexander—the policeman
sauntered up to the house
about tea time, followed by
a damp subdued little pig.
I disposed of Alexander in
the neighbourhood; he did
fairly well when he had
settled down.

Pigling Bland went on
alone dejectedly; he came
to cross-roads and a sign-
post—'To Market Town, 5
miles,' 'Over the Hills, 4 miles,' 'To Pettitoes Farm, 3 miles.'

Pigling Bland was shocked, there was little hope of sleeping in
Market Town and to-morrow was the hiring fair; it was deplorable
to think how much time had been wasted by the frivolity of
Alexander.

He glanced wistfully along the road towards the hills, and then
set off walking obediently the other way, buttoning up his coat
against the rain. He had never wanted to go; and the idea of
standing all by himself in a crowded market, to be stared at,
pushed, and hired by some big strange farmer was very disagree-
able—

'I wish I could have a little garden and grow potatoes,' said
Pigling Bland.

He put his cold hand in his pocket and felt his paper, he put his other hand in his other pocket and felt another paper—Alexander's! Pigling squealed; then ran back frantically, hoping to overtake Alexander and the policeman.

He took a wrong turn—several wrong turns, and was quite lost. It grew dark, the wind whistled, the trees creaked and groaned.

Pigling Bland became frightened and cried 'Wee, wee, wee! I can't find my way home!'

After an hour's wandering he got out of the wood; the moon shone through the clouds, and Pigling Bland saw a country that was new to him.

The road crossed a moor; below was a wide valley with a river twinkling in the moonlight, and beyond, in misty distance, lay the hills.

He saw a small wooden hut, made his way to it, and crept inside—'I am afraid it *is* a hen house, but what can I do?' said Pigling Bland, wet and cold and quite tired out.

'Bacon and eggs, bacon and eggs!' clucked a hen on a perch.

'Trap, trap, trap! cackle, cackle, cackle!' scolded the disturbed cockerel. 'To market, to market! jiggetty jig!' clucked a broody white hen roosting next to him. Pigling Bland, much alarmed, determined to leave at daybreak. In the meantime, he and the hens fell asleep.

In less than an hour they were all awakened. The owner, Mr. Peter Thomas Piperson, came with a lantern and a hamper to catch six fowls to take to market in the morning.

He grabbed the white hen roosting next to the cock; then his eye fell upon Pigling Bland, squeezed up in a corner. He made a singular remark—'Hallo, here's another!'—seized Pigling by the scruff of the neck, and dropped him into the hamper. Then he dropped in five more dirty, kicking, cackling hens upon the top of Pigling Bland.

The hamper containing six fowls and a young pig was no light weight; it was taken down hill, unsteadily, with jerks. Pigling, although nearly scratched to pieces, contrived to hide the papers and peppermints inside his clothes.

At last the hamper was bumped down upon a kitchen floor, the lid was opened, and Pigling was lifted out. He looked up, blinking, and saw an offensively ugly elderly man, grinning from ear to ear.

'This one's come of himself, whatever,' said Mr. Piperson, turning Pigling's pockets inside out. He pushed the hamper into a corner, threw a sack over it to keep the hens quiet, put a pot on the fire, and unlaced his boots.

Pigling Bland drew forward a coppy stool, and sat on the edge of it, shyly warming his hands. Mr. Piperson pulled off a boot and threw it against the wainscot at the further end of the kitchen. There was a smothered noise—'Shut up!' said Mr. Piperson. Pigling Bland warmed his hands, and eyed him.

Mr. Piperson pulled off the other boot and flung it after the first, there was again a curious noise—'Be quiet, will ye?' said Mr. Piperson. Pigling Bland sat on the very edge of the coppy stool.

Mr. Piperson fetched meal from a chest and made porridge. It seemed to Pigling that something at the further end of the kitchen was taking a suppressed interest in the cooking, but he was too hungry to be troubled by noises.

Mr. Piperson poured out three platefuls: for himself, for Pigling, and a third—after glaring at Pigling—he put away with much scuffling, and locked up. Pigling Bland ate his supper discreetly.

After supper Mr. Piperson consulted an almanac, and felt Pigling's ribs; it was too late in the season for curing bacon, and he grudged his meal. Besides, the hens had seen this pig.

He looked at the small remains of a flitch, and then looked undecidedly at Pigling. 'You may sleep on the rug,' said Mr. Peter Thomas Piperson.

Pigling Bland slept like a top. In the morning Mr. Piperson made more porridge; the weather was warmer. He looked to see how much meal was left in the chest, and seemed dissatisfied— 'You'll likely be moving on again?' said he to Pigling Bland.

Before Pigling could reply, a neighbour, who was giving Mr. Piperson and the hens a lift, whistled from the gate. Mr. Piperson hurried out with the hamper, enjoining Pigling to shut the door behind him and not meddle with nought; or 'I'll come back and skin ye!' said Mr. Piperson.

It crossed Pigling's mind that if *he* had asked for a lift, too, he might still have been in time for market.

But he distrusted Peter Thomas.

After finishing breakfast at his leisure, Pigling had a look round the cottage; everything was locked up. He found some potato peelings in a bucket in the back kitchen. Pigling ate the peel, and washed up the porridge plates in the bucket. He sang while he worked—

'Tom with his pipe made such a
noise,
He called up all the girls and
boys—
'And they all ran to hear him
play
'"Over the hills and far away!"'

Suddenly a little smoth-
ered voice chimed in—

'Over the hills and a great way
off,
The wind shall blow my top
knot off!'

Pigling Bland put down
a plate which he was wip-
ing, and listened.

After a long pause, Pig-
ling went on tip-toe and
peeped round the door into
the front kitchen. There was
nobody there.

After another pause, Pigling approached the door of the locked
cupboard, and snuffed at the keyhole. It was quite quiet.

After another long pause, Pigling pushed a peppermint under the door. It was sucked in immediately.

In the course of the day Pigling pushed in all the remaining six peppermints.

When Mr. Piperson returned, he found Pigling sitting before the fire; he had brushed up the hearth and put on the pot to boil; the meal was not get-at-able.

Mr. Piperson was very affable; he slapped Pigling on the back, made lots of porridge and forgot to lock the meal chest. He did lock the cupboard door; but without properly shutting it. He went to bed early, and told Pigling upon no account to disturb him next day before twelve o'clock.

Pigling Bland sat by the fire, eating his supper.

All at once at his elbow, a little voice spoke—'My name is Pig-wig. Make me more porridge, please!' Pigling Bland jumped, and looked round.

A perfectly lovely little black Berkshire pig stood smiling beside him. She had twinkly little screwed up eyes, a double chin, and a short turned up nose.

She pointed at Pigling's plate; he hastily gave it to her, and fled to the meal chest. 'How did you come here?' asked Pigling Bland.

'Stolen,' replied Pig-wig, with her mouth full. Pigling helped himself to meal without scruple. 'What for?

'Bacon, hams,' replied Pig-wig cheerfully. 'Why on earth don't you run away?' exclaimed the horrified Pigling.

'I shall after supper,' said Pig-wig decidedly.

Pigling Bland made more porridge and watched her shyly.

She finished a second plate, got up, and looked about her, as though she were going to start.

'You can't go in the dark,' said Pigling Bland.

Pig-wig looked anxious.

'Do you know your way by daylight?'

'I know we can see this little white house from the hills across the river. Which way are *you* going, Mr. Pig?'

'To market—I have two pig papers. I might take you to the bridge; if you have no objection,' said Pigling much confused and sitting on the edge of his coppy stool. Pig-wig's gratitude was such and she asked so many questions that it became embarrassing to Pigling Bland.

He was obliged to shut his eyes and pretend to sleep. She became quiet, and there was a smell of peppermint.

'I thought you had eaten them,' said Pigling, waking suddenly.

'Only the corners,' replied Pig-wig, studying the sentiments with much interest by the firelight.

'I wish you wouldn't; he might smell them through the ceiling,' said the alarmed Pigling.

Pig-wig put back the sticky peppermints into her pocket; 'Sing something,' she demanded.

'I am sorry ... I have toothache,' said Pigling much dismayed. 'Then I will sing,' replied Pig-wig. 'You will not mind if I say iddy tidditty? I have forgotten some of the words.'

Pigling Bland made no objection; he sat with his eyes half shut, and watched her.

She wagged her head and rocked about, clapping time and singing in a sweet little grunty voice—

' A funny old mother pig lived in a
    stye, and three little piggies had she;
' (Ti idditty idditty) umph, umph,
    umph! and the little pigs said,
    wee, wee!'

She sang successfully through three or four verses, only at every verse her head nodded a little lower, and her little twinkly eyes closed up.

' Those three little piggies grew peaky and lean, and lean they might very well be;
' For somehow they couldn't say umph, umph, umph! and they wouldn't say wee, wee, wee!
' For somehow they couldn't say—

Pig-wig's head bobbed lower and lower, until she rolled over, a little round ball, fast asleep on the hearth-rug.

Pigling Bland, on tip-toe, covered her up with an antimacassar.

He was afraid to go to sleep himself; for the rest of the night he sat listening to the chirping of the crickets

and to the snores of Mr. Piperson overhead.

Early in the morning, between dark and daylight, Pigling tied up his little bundle and woke up Pig-wig. She was excited and half-frightened.

'But it's dark! How can we find our way?'

'The cock has crowed; we must start before the hens come out; they might shout to Mr. Piperson.'

Pig-wig sat down again, and commenced to cry.

'Come away Pig-wig; we can see when we get used to it. Come! I can hear them clucking!'

Pigling had never said shuh! to a hen in his life, being peaceable; also he remembered the hamper.

He opened the house door quietly and shut it after them. There was no garden; the neighbourhood of Mr. Piperson's was

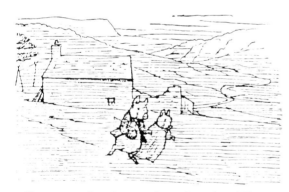

all scratched up by fowls. They slipped away hand in hand across an untidy field to the road.

The sun rose while they were crossing the moor, a dazzle of light over the tops of the hills. The sunshine crept down the slopes into the peaceful green valleys, where little white cottages nestled in gardens and orchards.

'That's Westmorland,' said Pig-wig. She dropped Pigling's hand and commenced to dance, singing—

'Tom, Tom, the piper's son, stole a pig
    and away he ran!
'But all the tune that he could play,
    was "Over the hills and far away!"'

'Come, Pig-wig, we must get to the bridge before folks are stirring.' 'Why do you want to go to market, Pigling?' inquired Pig-wig presently. 'I don't want; I want to grow potatoes.' 'Have a peppermint?' said Pig-wig. Pigling Bland refused quite crossly. 'Does your poor toothy hurt?' inquired Pig-wig. Pigling Bland grunted.

Pig-wig ate the peppermint herself and followed the opposite side of the road. 'Pig-wig! keep under the wall, there's a man ploughing.' Pig-wig crossed over, they hurried down hill towards the county boundary.

Suddenly Pigling stopped; he heard wheels.

Slowly jogging up the road below them came a tradesman's cart. The reins flapped on the horse's back, the grocer was reading a newspaper.

'Take that peppermint out of your mouth, Pig-wig, we may have to run. Don't say one word. Leave it to me. And in sight of the bridge!' said poor Pigling, nearly crying. He began to walk frightfully lame, holding Pig-wig's arm

The grocer, intent upon his newspaper, might have passed them, if his horse had not shied and snorted. He pulled the cart crossways, and held down his whip. 'Hallo! Where are *you* going to?'—Pigling Bland stared at him vacantly.

'Are you deaf? Are you going to market?' Pigling nodded slowly.

'I thought as much. It was yesterday. Show me your licence?'

Pigling stared at the off hind shoe of the grocer's horse which had picked up a stone.

The grocer flicked his whip—'Papers? Pig licence?' Pigling fumbled in all his pockets, and handed up the papers. The grocer read them, but still seemed dissatisfied.

'This here pig is a young lady; is her name Alexander?' Pig-wig opened her mouth and shut it again; Pigling coughed asthmatically.

The grocer ran his finger down the advertisement column of his newspaper—'Lost, stolen or strayed, 10s. reward.' He looked suspiciously at Pig-wig. Then he stood up in the trap, and whistled for the ploughman.

'You wait here while I drive on and speak to him,' said the grocer, gathering up the reins. He knew that pigs are slippery; but surely, such a *very* lame pig could never run!

'Not yet, Pig-wig, he will look back.' The grocer did so; he saw the two pigs stock-still in the middle of the road. Then he looked over at his horse's heels; it was lame also; the stone took some time to knock out, after he got to the ploughman.

'Now, Pig-wig, NOW!' said Pigling Bland.

Never did any pigs run as these pigs ran! They raced and squealed and pelted down the long white hill towards the bridge. Little fat Pig-wig's petticoats fluttered, and her feet went pitter, patter, pitter, as she bounded and jumped.

They ran, and they ran, and they ran down the hill, and across a short cut on level green turf at the bottom, between pebble beds and rushes.

They came to the river, they came to the bridge—they crossed it hand in hand—then over the hills and far away she danced with Pigling Bland!